To Tamar Mays
—D.G.
To Ava and Noah
—T.B.

Rappy the Raptor
Text copyright © 2015 by Dan Gutman
Illustrations copyright © 2015 by Tim Bowers
All rights reserved. Manufactured in China. No part of this book may be used or reproduced
in any manner whatsoever without written permission except in the case of brief quotations
embodied in critical articles and reviews. For information address HarperCollins Children's
Books, a division of HarperCollins Publishers, 195 Broadway, New York, NY 10007.
www.harpercollinschildrens.com

Library of Congress Cataloging-in-Publication Data
Gutman, Dan.
  Rappy the raptor / by Dan Gutman ; illustrated by Tim Bowers. — First edition.
      pages cm
  Summary: "Rappy the Raptor tells the story of how he became a rapping velociraptor, all in
rhyme"— Provided by publisher.
  ISBN 978-0-06-229180-6 (hardcover)
  [1. Stories in rhyme. 2. Velociraptor—Fiction. 3. Dinosaurs—Fiction. 4. Rap (Music)—Fiction.
5. Medical care—Fiction.] I. Bowers, Tim, illustrator. II. Title.
  PZ8.3.G9638Rap 2015   2014005875
  [E]—dc23   CIP
                                                         AC

The artist used acrylic paint, using paintbrushes and a sponge on watercolor board,
to create the illustrations for this book.
Typography by Rick Farley
15 16 17 18 19 SCP 10 9 8 7 6 5 4 3 2 1
❖
First Edition

RAPPY
the
RAPTOR

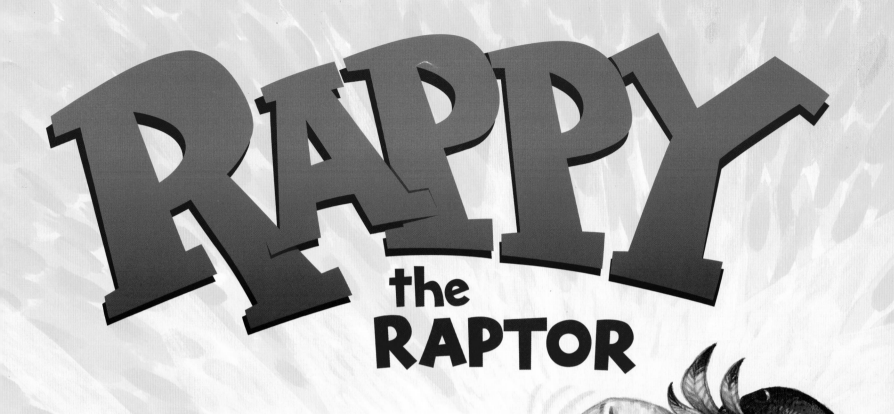

By Dan Gutman
Illustrated by Tim Bowers

HARPER
An Imprint of HarperCollinsPublishers

I'm Rappy the Raptor
and I'd like to say,
I may not talk in the usual way.

I'm rhymin' and rappin'
all of the time.
I'm talkin' when I'm walking
and I'm rhymin' when I climb.

I'm rappin' at my school
and I'm rappin' with my peeps.
Sometimes they even tell me
that I'm rappin' in my sleep.

Now, how did it happen
that I started rappin'?
Well, here's my story
in all its glory!

I was born in a tree
back in Memphis, Tennessee.
My mom (that's Mappy)
and my dad (that's Pappy)
took one look at me
and got oh so happy!

When I popped from my egg,
hip-hoppin' on my leg,
I tried to fly
(and I don't know why),
but the next thing I knew,
I was falling from the sky!

I landed on a shed
and I smacked my head.
I turned all red.
I had to go to bed!

But here's the big surprise:
When I opened up my eyes,
I was feeling just fine,
and I was talking in rhyme!

I'm Rappy the Raptor
and I'd like to say,
I may not talk in the usual way.

I'm rappin' in the morning,
I'm rappin' at noon.
I'm rappin' in October
and I'm rappin' in June.

My parents freaked out;
they didn't know what to do.
Should they take me to the doctor?
Or take me to the zoo?

They rushed me to the hospital;
the ambulance was screaming.
The nurse gave me a Popsicle;
I thought that I was dreaming!

The doctors looked me in the eye
and looked me in the ear.
And I'm not ashamed to say
they even looked me in the rear.